I'M SUPPOSED TO BE KING BUT MY MOM SAID NO!
Copyright © 2022 by James Jackson & Jennifer Jackson Nkansah
Library of Congress Control Number: 2022903529
ISBN: 979-8-9856819-2-5 (Paperback)

I'm Supposed To Be King But My Mom Said No!

Written by:
James Jackson &
Jennifer Jackson Nkansah

Illustrated by:

—105—
PUBLISHING
EST. 2020

This is dedicated to my inspirations. Mom, you taught me how to be a mother. Dad, for years we planned on writing this together and we did it! Maxwell, my husband; my Ohene, Sophiah, my Joy; King James, the son who warms my heart.

Acknowledgments

I would like to acknowledge everyone who has contributed to our beautiful family in any way. I thank the Creator for filling me with gifts that I get to share. Also I would like to thank Charmain for listening to decades of stories from the salon chair. Thank you Heather for loving my children and caring for them so willingly. Thank you to those who helped me see and harness my creativity; Uncle Trent, James V., Heather C., Lainie F., Amber W., Jennifer R., Jami H., and many others. Thank you to my bestie and sis, Jazmin for believing in me no matter how lofty my goal or lengthy the journey. To my muses Donna and James Jackson: You are now in spirit and I feel you with me; filling me with inspiration, laughter and memories of the best childhood a girl could have wanted, thank you. To my children, my wings: You bring me so much laughter, joy and inspiration. My life is what it is because I get to hold you, learn from you, and love you every day. Finally, thank you to my husband Maxwell Nkansah. You know me, support me, celebrate with me, and make this life exciting and good.

It was a Fursday, I think, or maybe Sunday. I picked out gray pants, a blue shirt (because blue is my favorite color), and my favorite tie with stripes to wear that day.

Dad, mom, sister, and I went to visit my Umpa (Grandpa) and Nana (Grandma) at their blue house. I like their house because I have lots of places to hide.

I hide behind the couch in the living room. I like to hide in the bathroom behind the door. Sometimes I try to hide upstairs if a grown-up doesn't stop me first.

My favorite place to hide is under the kitchen table. I can see and hear everything, but no one can see me!

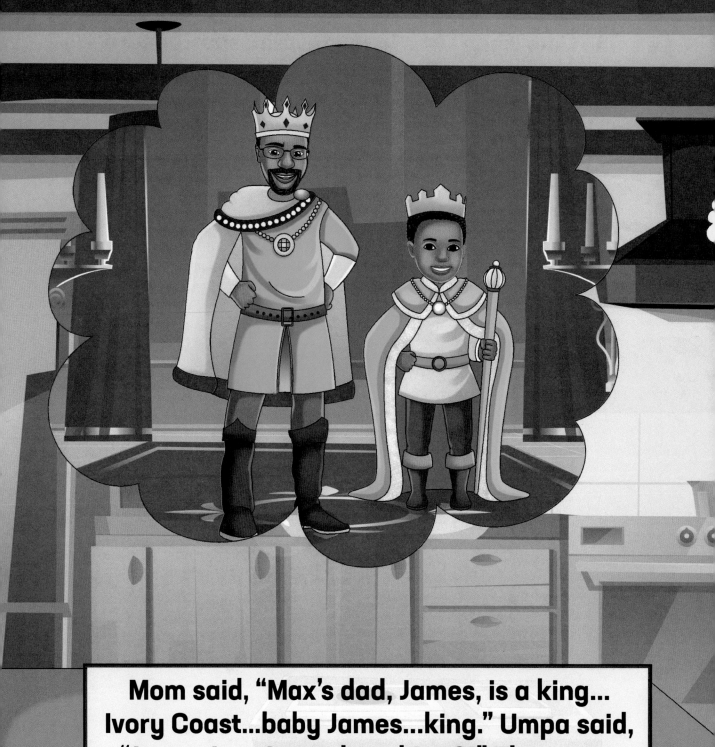

Mom said, "Max's dad, James, is a king...
Ivory Coast...baby James...king." Umpa said,
"James is going to be a king?!" Then mom
said, "He is supposed to be king, but I say
NO!" Then they laughed and talked about
my sister's birthday wishes.

Did you hear that? I am supposed to be a king, but my mom said NO.

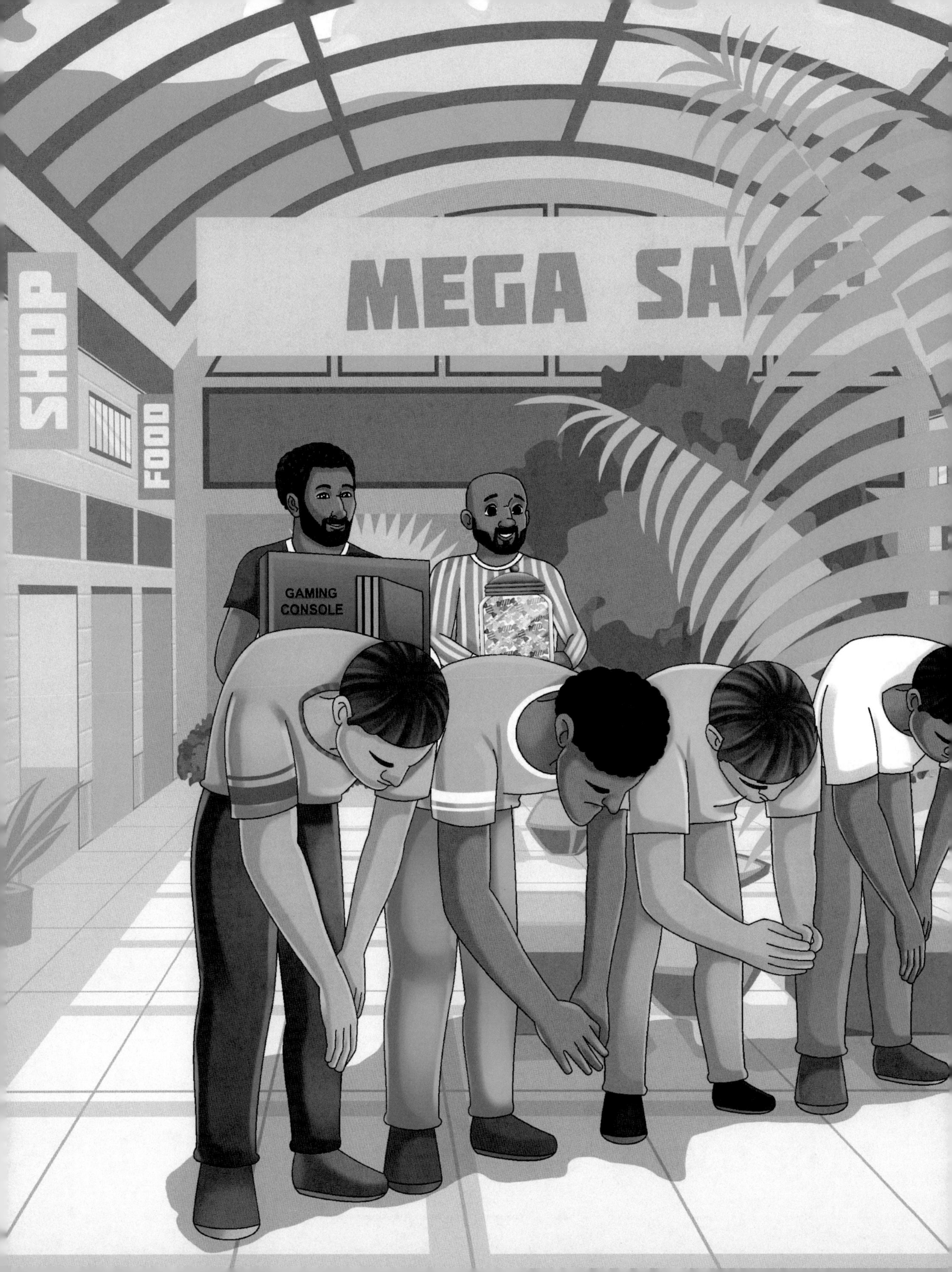
MEGA
SHOP
FOOD
GAMING
CONSOLE

If I were a king, no one would stop me from being king. I would go places, eat treats, and have an adventure every day!

Every king has clothes that make him look like a king. I would wear a blue shirt, gray pants, and my favorite tie.

My cape would be turquoise, because turquoise is another one of my favorites. My shoes would be green. I like green.

Before each adventure, I would put up my hand and say, "I am King James!"

The first thing I would do as King James is fly around the world. So, LET'S GO!

THE END

About the Author

Jennifer Jackson Nkansah was born and raised in Michigan and now lives with her family in North Carolina. She has enjoyed writing for years and has a self-care book called *Let's Table this Discussion: True Talk with Heart Friends*, which was self-published in 2020. This is Jennifer's first debut children's book published by 105 Publishing.

For twenty years, Jennifer was a college professor and taught Communication, Interpersonal Communication, Conflict Resolution, Intercultural Communication and Public Speaking. In her second career as a licensed counselor, Jennifer runs a private practice, *Inkansah Counseling, pllc*. She works with clients ages 13 and up. She is a nationally board certified counselor, brainspotting consultant, certified practitioner, and certified life coach.

Jennifer is a professional singer who enjoys reading, learning, and collecting crystals as well as laughing with her husband and children.

105 Publishing LLC
Austin, Texas
www.105publishing.com